WELCOME to the last part of One Eye

Grey for 2007. An issue that comes alive outside the M25, but even if some of the action takes place beyond the city, London runs through it like, er, Brighton through the rock. One place that sadly you won't be able to run through by the time you read this is the peerless New Piccadilly Café of Denman Street that shut it doors in September. Not that Lorenzo and the others really ever encouraged running on the premises, particularly after a heavy pudding. As well as puddings it was the purveyor of an excellent egg and chips and displayer of some truly odd waiter's uniforms. It will be sorely missed.

Now onto something at least as dreadful as the news of the Piccadilly's closure, the final installment of One Eye Grey for 2007. In this one we couldn't find room for Carl's adventures in Great Yarmouth so that story is available free online at www.fandmpublications.co.uk. Also available from us (with a free mystery book) for £9.00 are the collected 2007 set. We think it would make someone the ideal Christmas gift. We're not sure who, but someone.

We hope to be back next year with new writers, new stories, new illustrators. Just new basically. We aim to have the first of 2008 out by April and feature tales of Eskimo infants haunting Nine Elms and a bizarre parallel London where the zoo in SE17 makes Walworth the playground of the rich and famous whilst Primrose Hill festers in poverty and violence. But until then, when Elephants fly, enjoy this final selection for 2007 which features for illustration that most awful of things, the British coastal resort out of season.

OUT OF THE ORBITAL

J ust because you'd tired of London, it didn't mean you'd tired of life. I had, however, become weary of my London life. There were some things I'd known I'd miss, of course, like the South Bank on a Sunday with its strolling lovers, the celeb twitchers outside ITV and the superb budgie man. I had indulged in one last act of random surrealism in attending a festival of light in Myatts Field (an oxymoron in itself) then, returning home, had climbed up to my tenement roof to gaze at Big Ben through the Dick Van Dyke skyscape. After that, I'd forced myself to concentrate on all the things no one should have to put up with. Leading the field was the supermarket experience on the Walworth Road, where the only consistent special promotion was the offer of two-for-one nutters in the queue. Then I dwelt upon the thought that never again would my journeys be interrupted by the guy handing out leaflets saying 'Abu Shanti Brixton', and the staff at the Fish Bar would be gifted no more opportunities to sneeze into my tea.

Disappearing was not as easy as you'd think. Even if I maintained the will not to communicate, there would always be the random chance of meeting some echo of my past in the most unlikely places. After all, it wasn't as if I was going to try a Reggie Perrin (or John Stonehouse) and leave my clothes on a beach somewhere. Nor would I take the easier option (which people suspected of me) and flee abroad to wander the ashrams of India, the temples of the Incas or the Thai beaches. I agreed with the Alabama 3 on that point – I

certainly wasn't going to Goa. I'd find my redemption at home. Well
– close to home, anyway. I was simply going to refuse to cross the
orbital, however close I came on occasion. I would circle its exterior,
exploring the outer moons of the metropolis.

Before that had come the catharsis of packing. It was such a
liberating experience that I found myself wishing I'd done it sooner.
There was simply no avoiding it; clothes, furniture, talismanic sou-
venirs, all went in the purge; there was no time for a gentle setting
aside. Some people even did rather well out of it. Those of my more
important possessions that I wasn't taking with me were swallowed
by the under-stair storage space at Sally's. So, while I wasn't quite
a vagrant with a knotted cloth at the end of a stick, I certainly carried fewer possessions into my new life than I'd lived with in the
previous one.

Perhaps it was foolish, but also inevitable, that I first washed up
at that halfway house where all arrive who have wearied of London
and yet are unable to let it go. Brighton was Camden by the sea,
a city (now) with its posher Siamese twin, Hove. Together they
attracted the stars and dreamers and idlers and maladjusted. Just like
the north London therapy belt, it got the gays, the goths, the new
age buffs and would-be rag-trade entrepreneurs. Despite all that, I
liked it there more than I'd expected to. I loved the slight seediness
that the council was determined to erase and the architecture and
open skies. I also cherished the slower pace, and swimming in the
sea instead of a lido. There was a sense that nothing was too far away
to reach easily, using the charming buses named after local celebrities.
A person could lose oneself here, at least a little. Or so I thought.

Naturally, there were whispers from the larger settlement up
the railway. Free papers trashed up the trains, the London Evening
Standard and Time Out were available in shops, and great waves

of metropolitans flooded down on summer weekends. Despite this, Brighton had its own identity and lacked the subservience to London that other settlements had. In its own way, it was a fashion leader and an example to other towns. When I arrived, I was amused to find that Brighton and Hove were celebrating old age, just as all the other south coast resorts were trying to copy their success in capturing the young. Brighton, always a leap ahead, knew that youth was wasted on the middle aged and that it was foolish to rely on the belly pierced and t-shirt market forever

Through an employment agency, I found a job temping at the art college, filling in on their foundation course. In doing so, I'd struck up a friendship with the woman who'd set up the agency, Phyllis, a bit of sort in a busy kind of way – brunette, comfy cleavage, chatty manner and the positives that go with that. In another age and time she might have been a bartender. Here she ran, with pretty much the same skills, her own agency. She told me about a club, Catalyst, where people got to talk about their passions.

'It's great, you could get anything. Sex to Beethoven, Marmite, seventies detective shows, whatever excites the person giving the talk. Do you fancy coming along?'

I wasn't entirely sure that a club about obsessions was what I needed but I said yes anyway. I think she thought I needed cheering up. I think she thought, in that kindly way people have, that I'd be good for a pal of hers.

'Be nice to Mary, Carl. She had a bit of shock last year and I'm not sure she's fully over it yet,' Phyllis had said, with a warning in her voice that, although she liked me, others would always come first.

I smiled and thought to myself that we'd all had a shock last year. My new year's resolution certainly hadn't been to kill Martin.

HOME IS WHERE THE HEART IS

Mary Taylor Jones glanced around her living room, then out of the window and finally at the parcel in front of her. It was not Christmas, it certainly was not her birthday and yet this had come with the morning mail. She eyed it suspiciously, prodded it with a pencil and wondered what on earth it could be and whom on earth it could be from.

The item was about 18 inches square. It was quite solid, yet rattled softly if shaken. Mary did not like to do this too hard or often, however, in case she harmed something fragile within.

Eventually, after some careful consideration as to whether or not it might be dangerous, she decided it might be safe to open it. Mary could think of neither a terrorist organisation that wished her harm or that she might have offended, nor a politician whose name her own sounded even vaguely similar to. She discounted the fur coat she had inherited and, as far as she was aware, no one had issued a jihad on her, despite the unpopularity of her profession. Mary worked in property and had hoped to spend the early part of her day finishing some paperwork so she could enjoy the rest of the weekend. The package was an unlooked-for interruption.

At this point, the doorbell rang again. Putting aside the package, she got up to answer it. In front of the door stood a deliveryman.

'Is it your birthday?' he smiled, indicating a large, gaudily wrapped package on the floor. 'If you could just sign here for it, please,' he thrust a clipboard towards her.

'But I didn't order anything.' Her eyes widened with concern.

'Well, it is addressed to you. Look, there's the name and address,' he indicated the label. 'You don't know anyone else here by that name, do you?'

'No,' Mary replied meekly, wishing that she did.

She put the parcel down beside the other one. This second one was lighter and more flexible; something about it suggested clothing or, at any rate, fabric. Now there were two mysteries for her to ponder. She picked up the phone and dialled her friend Phyllis. It rang for some time before it was answered.

'Hi Phyllis, it's me, Mary. I don't know what to say, really, I have a slight dilemma on my hands... No, don't be silly, he's never been remotely interested since I told him about my ex's little accident... No, I know he was only expressing interest but I do think an engagement ring after one night out at the pictures is a bit strong. The problem is, I've been sent something... Well, I don't know, I haven't opened them yet... Yes, there's more than one. Oh Phyl, that's the door – can you hold the line a moment?'

Phyllis played with her hair, rubbed her eyes and seriously questioned her friend's manners in calling on a Saturday morning at, what, 10.30? Mary's voice returned, now at a slightly higher pitch.

'Phyllis, are you there? This is insane! Another parcel's arrived, from a different courier company. The guy refused point blank to give me the name of the sender, he said it wasn't company policy. Is there some law about this? No, it is not my birthday. I am not the Queen and therefore I have one birthday, on April the 28th... What do you mean, just open them? There could be anything inside them! This last one weighs a ton, I think the courier was pretty mad that I didn't help him... Well, I know you should, but not for services you haven't requested. Look... do you think I should call the police?'

Mary paused, listening out for the door again.

'Well, no, Phyl, they don't look like bombs. But if they were, they wouldn't announce the fact, would they? It would ruin the point a bit. Besides which, I'm unaccustomed to receiving letter bombs, I wouldn't know what one looked like... No, they're neatly wrapped, with ribbons. I would say a woman packaged them, men are never up to much, gift-wrapping-wise. And the labels are typed... Yes, that's true, but I suppose if a man sent them he could have got a woman to parcel it up for him... The paper? Oh, quite lovely. Home-made, even. Like that has anything to do with it. Oh shit! Phyllis, that's the door again. Do you think you could come over? Well, you can bring him as well. Look, I have some food here, why not come over for lunch? In about an hour? Oh, and Phyllis – ring the door-bell three times, okay? Ciao.'

Mary put the phone down and went to the door, on the other side of which was another bundle.

'Look, I don't know who's sending these but I wish they'd stop.'

The delivery man looked at her uneasily. There was always the odd mad one who ordered things then forgot they'd done it. He had been warned at his induction training to be firm but polite. 'Just be on time and get them to sign' was the company motto, and he intended to do just that. Still, he didn't expect younger people to be difficult. The woman in front of him, dark, apparently affluent and well cared for, was not what he had in mind when the training officer had outlined problem customers. She was a shade skinny for his taste but a bit of a sort nevertheless. He considered that a bit of flattery might help.

'Er... Mrs Jones...'

'Miss Taylor Jones, please, and before you say another word I want you to know that I have phoned my lawyer and the police about these intrusions. They should be arriving soon. The police, that is,' Mary lied, badly.

Realising that charm would get him nowhere, the man resorted to a grimmer manner. 'That's just fine. If you'll sign here, I can be away before they get here. I'm just the errand boy, as it goes, so there's no point taking it out on me. Here is a card with our number on it. If you have any complaints, phone that. In the meantime, would you like me to carry this in?'

'No,' she snapped. 'Oh... yes! Over there by the sofa, please.' She indicated a space by the other parcels. Mary signed the pink slip and felt a little annoyed with herself for losing her temper.

'Happy birthday, Mrs... er, Miss...' was the man's parting shot.

'Thank you,' drawled Mary towards the closing door, thinking for the first time in many years how delicious a cigarette might be.

Phyllis got out of bed and stumbled into her bathroom, wondering how to explain the situation to the body she had in her bed. That her friends were mad and required her presence to open gifts? That she had a Saturday job caring for the insane? That she was eager to show him off? That she had forgotten the appointment?

The shower she stumbled into felt hot and good and clean. The coffee that followed was essential. The carcass in the bed stirred, blinked and was about to speak when he realised he was alone.

'Phyl? Are you there?' he called.

She emerged, leisurely clad in Lycra and bearing a cup of coffee.

'Listen,' she breathed, 'are you hungry? Okay, good, get dressed, a friend of mine is cooking lunch. I know, I'd have liked to stay in bed too but it's her birthday. No, you don't know her. It's just that I promised I'd pop round. It won't be for very long. Besides, you'll like me better if I keep you away from my cooking for as long as possible.'

Mary began preparing lunch. It got her out of the front room, at least, where four bundles now lay in various accusing positions. The kitchen door was firmly shut against them and the noise of hissing gas and clattering pans provided a pleasant diversion from the collection of unwelcome arrivals next door. By the time Phyllis appeared, Mary had done her best to forget about the ribbons and home-made paper and tetchy delivery men. But crossing the room to open the door reminded her.

'Hi Mary, happy birthday! Did you get what I sent you?' Phyllis said with a wink. 'Mary this is Geoff, Geoff this is Mary!'

'Happy birthday, Mary. Sorry I haven't got you anything.'

Mary shot Phyllis a dark look and said, 'Oh, don't worry about it. Come in please, sit down if you can find a space.'

'You must be awfully popular,' observed Geoff, helpfully.

'It would appear so,' Mary answered coolly. 'If you'll excuse me for a minute, I've just got to finish up in the kitchen. Would you like anything to drink?'

'Sure, what do you have?' enquired Geoff, before noticing some blank expressions and adding, 'Would you like me to go out for anything?'

'Oh, yes! Would you be an angel and get something sparkling? There's an off-licence on the corner,' suggested Phyllis.

After Geoff had gone, she turned to Mary.

'Isn't he a doll?'

Mary nodded, 'Absolutely!' before gesturing towards the boxes and saying, 'What the hell does this mean?'

'I don't know. Have you opened any yet?'

'No. I was waiting for you to get here. Oh no, that's the door again. Look, could you get it? If it's a delivery service, tell them

I'm not in. I thought they stopped working on Saturday afternoons anyway.'

'Yeah, sure I will. But it's probably Geoff, he's hopeless with directions, I'm afraid. A sweetie to look at but not the brightest star in the cosmos.'

Mary caught the conversation at the door. 'No,' Phyllis was saying, 'I'm not Mary, she's quite overcome with all the gifts, if you'll just permit me to sign. Thank you.'

Two more boxes arrived, one large and one small and both with very glitzy wrapping. Clutching her head, Mary screamed.

'What is this?'

'Well, there's only one way to find out. I know size isn't everything but I'll take the larger one if you can handle this,' Phyllis said, tossing the smaller of the packages towards Mary, who fielded it onto the sofa as one might a contagion. It landed with a thud against the leather upholstery.

'Careful, you might break it! God this ribbon is tough. Have you got any scissors? Thanks, that's better. Good lord, what is it?' The wrapping seemed to shimmer away of its own accord to reveal a thin cardboard box, inside which was a replica, in plywood, of a house.

'What's this? You're a bit old for dolls, aren't you Mary? What's in yours?'

The smaller package was surprisingly heavy, now that Mary came to pick it up. Opening it was easy enough, though. So easy, in fact, that the contents slipped through Mary's fingers and fell to the floor, where they glistened unpleasantly. It was a reproduction of the same house, in this case cast in glass. After a brief pause, the two friends started tearing into the remaining parcels, throwing paper everywhere and tossing the ribbons aside in an orgy of enquiry. Each gift contained a likeness of the house in a variety of materials including fabric, metal and pottery, and there was even a paper one that nearly got destroyed in the unwrapping. There was a note attached to the metal house that bore the legend, 'Home is Where the Heart Is.'

'What in heaven's name does that mean?'

Before Mary could reply, Geoff returned.

'Well, you might have waited!' he said, on seeing the mayhem. 'I guess you had a good time, though. Hey, Mary, do you collect houses or something?'

'Not exactly, darling, Mary is a mortgage advisor.'

'Actually, I got promoted to repossessions. But that's neither here nor there. Come on, let's eat,' Mary suggested, by way of changing the subject.

The reason Mary wanted to divert her guests was that she recognised the house portrayed in the presents. It was one she had arranged the mortgage for, years before. The couple who had bought it had been young, one a freelance designer the other a teacher. They had been delighted with the place and had taken out a most stringent policy in order to get it. Mary had pushed them along, despite some reservations on the husband's part about their ability to pay, especially as his wife was some months pregnant at the time.

Geoff had bought champagne to go with the food, or at least the closest the corner off licence could offer. It complemented the food fairly well, which was a simple dish of chicken and side salad. Mary ate sparingly, however, while the other two tucked in. The phrase on the note troubled her; it was one that she had used heavily in her sales pitch, to play on the devotion the couple clearly felt for each other, not to mention the desperation she picked up from the wife. Another thought, of a more pedestrian nature, was also troubling her; she hadn't prepared dessert for her guests. Excusing herself, she went to search the freezer for possibilities.

While she was doing this, the doorbell rang again. Phyllis answered it and was not surprised to find another courier waiting there. By now quite accustomed to opening the parcels, Phyllis tore into it and was pleased to find it contained a cake.

Geoff was very impressed with the creation, and even more so with the timing. He marvelled at the detail of the cake, with its solid white walls and bright red roof. Even the garden was exquisitely carved. And on the roof was inscribed the words: 'Home is Where the Heart Is'.

'Hey, Mary!' Phyllis called. 'Look, dessert on tap!'

Mary stared, somewhat aghast, but Geoff, by now relaxed by the champagne, asked if he could have a slice. Mary just nodded and passed him a knife.

'No, wait,' he said. 'It's your day, you cut it.'

Reluctantly, Mary took the blade and sliced into the roof. It was tougher than she might have expected but eventually she plunged through the icing, and screamed as red liquid flowed down the white walls and poured along the garden path towards the tiny gate.

Geoff fought the urge to vomit, Phyllis turned a pale shade of green and Mary passed out. The room stank of blood.

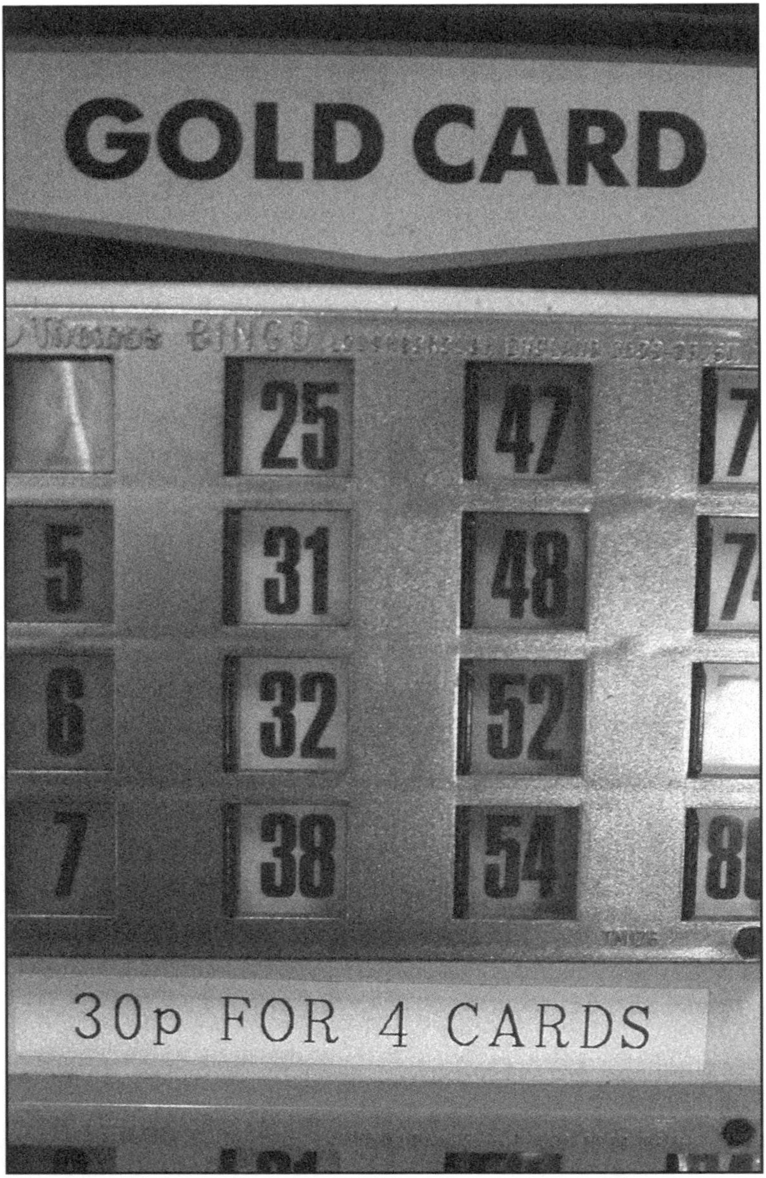
GOLD CARD
25
47
5
31
48
6
32
52
7
38
54
30p FOR 4 CARDS

A PROVINCIAL TOWN

I GOT ON WELL WITH PHYLLIS'S MATE MARY, WHO WORKED IN property. She hadn't seemed nervous or damaged at all, but I did get the story of what had shocked her so much. She'd been the recipient of an odd revenge plot from someone she'd sold a house to. A complete fruitcake by the name of Kate, who had later drowned herself and her child on the shore beyond the Marina where the under-cliff path leads to Rottingdean. I knew the spot exactly, it was where the girls from Roedean approached the small beaches via a Blytonesque tunnel under the cliff-top road. The bodies had been found by the school's first field trip of the day, not far from the tunnel. I could easily imagine the calls home that night. ('Mummy! You'll never guess!')

I'd been lost in that thought for a while when I realised that Phyllis was continuing the tale.

'It took a while for us to piece the story together, but it seemed that the woman was at her tethers end with mortgage repayments and wanted to make some sort of dramatic gesture. Temperamental, these artists. But you seem very measured,' she told me, incorrectly but reassuringly, patting my arm as she did so. I was torn between asking for more details and keeping quiet, because the juxtaposition of the name Kate and the phrase 'dramatic gesture' brought back a conversation from my final night out in Gerrard Street.

I could remember having entering a little reverie about how much I liked my crowd and how I saw them too infrequently. I recalled the name of Kate Harrison coming up, and Poppy getting quite vicious at the suggestion that Kate should have been invited to Martin's funeral. I had observed that Martin was not really that taken with vicar's-fete Kate but that he did like studying her eccentricities.

There was no doubt that Kate Harrison had talents but, like Salvadore Dali, she couldn't face her limitations as a visionary artist and had turned her skills to bizarre ends, seeking to shock and revolt rather than stimulate thought or joy. I now remembered the fake foetuses she'd positioned in public places for her final year project. I could also dimly call to mind a considerable aptitude for baking. So, it appeared that Kate had loosened all her abilities on poor Mary. I wondered if it was worth telling Omar that two-and-eight Kate never went north after all.

In the months I was there, Brighton kept doing that to me. Even out of season there were little echoes of London, an overheard conversation, a smell, even a way of walking. Occasionally, I'd spot someone I vaguely knew – a whoring journalist out on a jolly, TV presenter Pearl down for a hen night, others there for concerts, shopping or even a dip in the sea. It was, after all, only fifty minutes from Victoria. Too close, I thought. Just that bit too close.

Worthing, on the other hand, held no such attractions for the metropolitans and it had the advantage of cheaper rents. I could even live alone there, which was good. Not only because of my increasing misanthropy but also because flat-shares – when did 'to flat' become a verb? – are not good after the age of thirty. I thought of my ex-housemates and recalled that people who use the words 'grass roots' are usually not to be trusted with other people's belongings. And the poor girl who always got her washing wrong. She had yet to learn that you can never disguise the smell of imperfectly dried laundry, and that it smells of pov. For a time, I fondly considered my old home in SE11, which I'd sublet with little intention of going back. The lump sum pay-off-come-deposit I'd got from that had helped launch me into this journey, which I'd thought would take me to Wales or even Scotland. Right now, though, I hovered in the south east, hugging the rim of the Home Counties, exploring the washed-up fishing villages-turned-resorts converted into retirement homes and did, at least in Worthing, have a small home of my own.

I'd only been to Worthing once before. Years ago, to see The Fall who'd arrived late, Mark E Smith drunk beyond all ability. After half a song – Fiery Jack, I believe – he collapsed onto the stage and stayed there. Bottles, cans and all kinds of other portable objects began to be thrown, whereupon he roused himself on to one elbow, looked at the crowd and croaked.

'Just remember you're only a provincial town.'

That was the end of the concert, but he was right. The town was prosperous enough but had that air of being a place that was close to great things yet just too far away to touch them. Frustration throbbed from the old (who might have preferred Marbella), the young (who would have chosen London) and the young professionals (who secretly favoured Hove, however much they might have boosted Worthing in public). I quite liked it, though, and soon found myself indulging in a couple of old habits. The first of these was collecting trivial information. I'd already heard the story about this town, population 100,000, having the third busiest crematorium in Europe, attached to other of God's waiting rooms. More unique was the fact that the town is home to the English Bowling Association.

At times, I was reminded of my favourite London area, Pimlico, with its charity shops, old style Indian restaurants (cream of mushroom soup, mild curry and tinned fruit lunchtime specials) and slightly bewildered old folk visiting both. Thrift stores are always plentiful in retirement areas, with their high turnover of population and dead man's coats aplenty. The best I found was the Sussex Canine Welfare Society, which combined the excellence of a high-end Oxfam in terms of quality of clothes, and the peculiar quirkiness that only a local organisation can offer. A robust granny, Mrs Phillips, ran it most days, with a coterie of other matriarchs to back her up.

It was through Mrs Phillips that I first heard of the strange phenomenon of dogs disappearing in the night, and sometimes the day as well. As the shop was the hub of canine culture in the area, it was not surprising that reports of missing dogs should be particularly noted there and the volume was beginning to alarm the volunteers. Their response of some to the perceived crisis was also indicative of a town that in the 1930s boasted a Blackshirt councillor; rumours of gypsy encampments and peculiar ingredients turning up in Asian restaurants were aired. While I could agree to the latter (though I doubted it was dog being added to the Madras), one had to question whether even the most desperate band of pikeys could find a use for Mrs Neilson's elderly poodle.

There had been outbreaks of dog disappearances in previous decades. Now it was happening again. No blackmail letters were ever received, so it seemed clear that the dogs were being used for something. Two of the sillier theories could be dismissed, there being no evidence of sweatshops churning out hound-hide coats or illicit shampoo-testing laboratories in the borough.

To the west and north of the borough was some of the last remaining ancient woodland on the Sussex coastal plain, Titnore, bordering the larger Clapham Woods on the Downs. There had been a concentration of disappearances in and around the latter, and some owners reported that, even on a leash, their animals behaved strangely there. I'd been myself a couple of times and had once picked blackberries in the Clapham churchyard but had been too scared to eat dead man's berries and instead left them as a kind of sub-voodoo offering to one of the graves. The woods were quite tidy, and pathways led through them to the Arundal Road. In a few spots, fires had clearly been lit and there were strange stone arrangements. As an urban dweller for so much of my life, I instinctively found the woods a bit alarming and was confused about when and how to greet the fellow ramblers I ran into. On my many trips to London's enclosed green spaces, I rarely struck up conversations with strangers. Perhaps that was one of the things wrong with the place.

I seemed to be devoting more and more time to noting down what I felt was bad about London. Half of these jottings (one such entry ran Oysters and carnivals are the new bread and circuses) made no sense, even to me. It was in Worthing that I started writing in the way that people do when they need to get a grip on their life. Lettering as therapy, putting down my thoughts and experiences in the hope that they would reveal some sort of pattern that would magically make sense of life. I feared my nomadic drift and pondered on the murder I'd committed. I thought, too, of the life and lives I'd left behind to begin my journey.

I had no illusion that anything would come of my scribbles. I did not anticipate emulating Oscar Wilde, who wrote The Importance of Being Earnest in Worthing in 1884, or Harold Pinter, who scripted the Homecoming while living there. This material was, for me, just a means of maintaining a grip, holding onto some sort of memory of my actions and thoughts.

So I walked a lot at weekends, in the countryside and along the seafront where David Leland had filmed Wish You Were Here, a slogan I disagreed with. I didn't, for the moment, want anyone there, and wandered the town with an increasing sense that someone must be feeding off the despair and isolation that I, and others in the town, felt.

THORNS AROUND ENGLAND'S ROSE

Petra lay paralysed in the bushes. She could hear her mistress call, could even tantalisingly smell her when she came close, but couldn't move her mouth to communicate, couldn't struggle to a more visible spot in the hope of being found. It was agony for Petra as the anxious voice became quieter and the scent extinct as her mistress moved further and further away, yelling her name but in increasingly widening circles. Don't leave me here, come back, I want to go home, she thought. I want my ball, I want my bowl and basket, I even want one more go at getting the neighbour's cat. At least, if she had been human, that's how her thoughts might have run, alongside other questions such as How did this happen? and Why can't I move a muscle? One minute, she'd been happily running along ahead of her mistress. She'd veered off to investigate a strange aroma and had gone some way into the brambles when she'd felt a sharp nip in her hindquarters, and collapsed.

Being a corgi dog, Petra's thoughts weren't as tangible as that. They were a confused series of wants and needs, and some idea that these could be met if the situation was different, if she could just move or bark. She could hear other movements in the forest, the birds and small mammals, the soft rustle of the leaves in the slight wind. Then a thump, followed by heavy footsteps and a scent that was vaguely familiar. The footsteps came closer until they stopped behind her. Petra was lifted up and placed into a rough sack, and felt herself being carried some distance. Eventually she was dropped

– though not released – in quieter surroundings where there were none of the forest's usual sounds, and no wind. She was still in the woods but, somehow, inside. The man (and Petra knew it was man) who had carried her lit a cigarette – hand-rolled, by the smell of it – then spoke, although Petra could sense no one else nearby.

'It's all sorted for tomorrow night.' A pause, then, 'No, don't worry about that. Just let people know. I'll prepare everything at this end and I think the old flint mine in the western copse will be the best place, considering the alignments.' Another pause, then, 'I know the original idea was the white birch deadfall but we've used it too much recently.'

Inside the sack, Petra felt another sharp nip. This time, she lost all consciousness.

The woods were a different place after dark, particularly the central and inaccessible spots, but the people moving through it knew their way. Heavy feet converged on the agreed spot, treading the sinister tracks and rabbit paths.

Petra was awake again, hungry and frightened. Even inside the sack, she could feel the coolness in the air. The man had just returned and she caught his teasingly familiar scent, and the waft of tobacco. He stopped near the sack and Petra caught the stronger aroma of his boots. Searching for associations, she finally came to the realisation that this was the man who sometimes dropped paper through the box in their front door. In her doggy brain, of course, she had no concept of postman, just a linking of the scent to something she knew. The man lifted the sack that contained Petra to his shoulders, and Petra caught other smells now and when she was put down again of many people, but none of them familiar.

That wasn't surprising. There would have been no reason for Petra to have visited the city trading floors, media offices or chambers where these people worked. Had Petra been able to read newspapers instead of ripping them up with her paws, she might have recognised the reality show contestant to the left or the financier in the centre. She sensed that these were powerful people, though, and that they were cruel, or at least determined. Among the gathering of the Order Tempalis Diana or Queen of Hearts cult as some knew it, there were some very high achievers in their fields. How much their strength of mind had propelled them to the top and how much it was related to their activities in Clapham Woods, even they couldn't tell for sure. This was just something they did; alongside being ruthless and clear-sighted individuals, they were members of an organisation whose fellowship was tightly controlled and highly secretive.

They arrived as individuals, couples or small groups from across the southern counties, and exchanged greetings as they prepared the area and waited for the others. There had to be twenty-three of them at the ritual, because that is the number of chaos and, despite the precise nature of the Order Tempalis Diana's service, they believed in the fundamental turbulence of life. They also credited their clarity of vision within that disorder as key to the order's success in rising above the confusion. It was the 23rd of the month and this coincided with a twenty-three degree lunar elevation, which meant that conditions were perfect – auspicious, even. The modern occultist shies away from words like auspicious, initiate or invocation, however, because, like everyone else, they have seen enough Hammer films to recognise a cliché.

Some of the group shivered slightly as they changed from their work clothes into the uniform of their order. No robes here, this sect favoured dark Paul Smith suits and crisp white shirts, open at the neck to reveal a silver pendant of curious yet simple design. The gentlemen wore dark brogues and the women court shoes. Hair was, where necessary, pulled back off the face and whatever disguises worn on the way there were temporarily discarded.

This openness among themselves was in direct contrast to the layers of mystery, inscrutability and disguise employed against outsiders as when they walked somewhere, they walked alone, following their own calendar and rituals. Although only twenty-three of them were permitted at any given service, there were other associates watching out for interlopers, willing, if necessary, to divert, waylay and even assault strangers who strayed too close to the chosen site in the flint mine at the edge of the woods. The more affluent cultists subsidised the local associates, who often worked in relatively low paid jobs but were necessary to set up the rituals and provide information about the area.

There were perhaps a dozen spots favoured by the group, all of which they were careful to cover up after ceremonies so they'd be hard to trace. Other societies used the woods ranging from badger watchers and UFO spotters to Wiccans and the Emo kids who ran their own cider-fuelled revelries in the forest.

Before the main ceremony began, a smaller group moved off to the side and began the sterling invocation, which they believed ensured their own and the group's continuing prosperity. The invocation was led by a slim blonde woman, better known for interviewing famous pop stars and politicians, who began:

'Money is only evil when it is static; cash is a spirit of movement.

For the nature of readies has changed from land to gold to paper to plastic,

Now it is pure number. It is our friend electric.'

The rest of the group joined in:

'We say this and believe it, this is no careless whisper. That money is of the nature of air not earth, a spirit of human invention, yet imbued like a god or demon with a life of its own. It is a living being with its own loves, hates, fears and desires that revels in movement, it dances on the sand, and only in movement can reproduce itself.

'When treasure is hoarded it slowly dies, like china in the hand, but when it moves it achieves orgasm and we must become channels for its transfer. For finance to love us we must become conduits for its movement.'

A little louder, the small congregation chanted:

'Invest in us mammon and we will give you life. We will show you a good time, too much worry will get you down. We will welcome you to our working.'

Their pitch rose as they intoned:

'Invest in us that we become great channels for your power. Empower us money and we, your worshippers, will give you life.'

Finally came a plea:

'Give us the money. Give us the fucking money!'

From this, one might think that the occultist and his currency are soon parted. In a sense, this was true, for, like pimps, criminals or even city youths with their mighty bonuses, the occultists did swiftly push away whatever financial reward came their way, spending it on luxuries, revels and debauches as if it was unclean, a shameful lust or forbidden hobby. Unlike criminals, though, they welcomed the associated tainting, and more rewards came in its stead, to be spread around like manure; money, like energy, was an eternal delight.

With exquisite timing, as the chant finished, the postman appeared and left the squirming bag at the edge of the clearing.

The last of the night's cohort had arrived and were changing their clothes, while others began to purify the site by sprinkling water, salt and wine around the perimeter. Three of party carefully released Petra from the sack and held her while a fourth washed her with spring water, poured salt on her head and rubbed oil into her back before fitting a choker around her neck.

On cue, the moon slid into view above the clearing and two members led the strongly protesting Petra on a silver lead into the clearing. Twenty of the group closed the circle behind them while the convener stood beside a crude, woven, wooden structure with five leather straps attached to it. The silver lead was attached to the largest of these at the bottom and pulled tightly whilst the other four were slipped around the dog's fore and hind legs making the animal secure, if uncomfortable. Petra howled in this upside down crucified position but the collar was just tight enough to prevent too much sound emerging. Over her noise, the leader set up a call and response prayer for the group.

Leader: Mistress of the higher mysteries and leader of the pack hear our prayer.

Group: Hear the prayer we howl to thee.

Leader: Queen of hearts and empress of the heavens grant us your power.

Group: Hear the prayer we howl to thee.

Leader: Incomparable lover and best dressed of the gods grant us your beauty.

Group: Hear the prayer we howl to thee.

Leader: Mother of riches grant us your bounty.

Group: Hear the prayer we howl to thee.

Leader: Mighty Diana accept our gift.

Group: Hear the prayer we howl to thee.

Most of the group kept up their refrain whilst the two who had led the dog into the centre now approached with silver cups. The leader sliced up through the dog's stomach up to the genitals. The cups were used to capture the blood whilst a third figure neatly removed the innards. A woman with a languid demeanour but lively intelligent eyes took out the still beating heart. This she held up, letting the moonlight catch it, turning around so every person in the circle got a glimpse of the heart. She then plunged it into her mouth and swallowed. Once this was done, the high priest severed the dog's head and held it aloft to the moon before placing it within a wooden box. He then uncovered an already prepared pit of lime and the remains of the animal were uncuffed and lowered into this. The altar was dismantled and symbolically placed around the area. The chanting cupbearers covered the pit over with soil and laid a small silver effigy just below the uppermost level. The chief said over the grave, 'May the soul of this creature roam forever with our mistress, be a faithful hunter for her in the dark forests and realms and be a reminder to her of our devotion to she whom the pack follows.'

The woman who had swallowed the dog's heart kissed each member of the assembly in turn. Her eyes shone with a feral beauty before she ripped open her top and exposing herself to the moon. She then squatted down, removed her underwear and urinated noisily on the grave. Another member walked up, ceremoniously placed a single rose, pink with a white underlay, and blew out the candles.

WELCOME TO DREAMLAND

WORTHING WAS A FALSE START IN MANY WAYS. IT WAS A LITTLE kick to the west when the tidal suck really wanted to pull me east to the Cinque Ports and sunken towns of the south coast, Rye, Hastings and Eastbourne. I was following the art trail to Margate, which juts out into the North Sea on the island that is no longer an island (Thanet). The painter Turner described the town as having the finest light in Europe and with its sandy beaches and it had once been the leading seaside resort for Londoners. Now pierless and battered, Margate looked like an appendage of New Cross, with boarded shops and Poundpullahs vying for space in the high street. It might have been the first resort to introduce donkey rides, in 1890, and the first to have deckchairs eight years later but it was late arriving at the 21st century solution to spannered towns: the art industry.

I had seen Tracy Emin's Cunt Vernacular and Top Spot, both of which were set in Margate. However, the last-resort option I had come for was a museum based on something less controversial, Turner's residency in Margate. The wisdom, in this age of global warming, of situating a major museum on this stretch of coast was another matter. A friend of Phyllis's ran a small agency in Canterbury, and needed some people with an art background to help on a documentary linked to the museum. And so, I was to be part of a reconnaissance crew, outriders of the propaganda funding war. Despite its college, Canterbury had failed to provide, or perhaps its potential workers just knew more than I did because, a fortnight after arriving in Margate, I was told that the funding had been pulled. When I heard that the director was to have been an old acquaintance, Dean, I smiled and realised this was probably the information that the canny Canterburyites had in their possession. They must have had the precious knowledge that Dean carried a large white seabird with him when it came to bursaries, and that any project associated with him could fold as badly as those early deckchairs.

This left me literally out on a limb in a town with a great future behind it, and which was desperately trying to catch up with places (Whitstable, Broadstairs) it had once despised. Phyllis and her friend from Canterbury felt terribly guilty about the situation and promised help. Specifically, the friend swore she would recommend me for place on a project in Great Yarmouth that was being co-ordinated by a friend of hers. This was heartening but that wouldn't be starting until the following year. In the meantime, here I was, near Bleak House and, more disturbingly, in a place eulogised by Chas and Dave, facing a very unpleasant Christmas. It was mid-November. The decorations would have been up in Regent Street for ages. All the decent venues booked for parties, events diaries long filled. I thought fondly of Soho on Christmas Eve, the emptying pubs after the retail rage was over. How a quiet calm would descend as one boozer after another you thought never closed would shut at 8 or 9 o'clock, the last desperate band of drinkers chasing each other in ever-decreasing circles until they sloped off home or, in my case, to my annual scheduled church visit. Midnight Mass at St Mary Newington was something to which even Sally could be dragged, to murder Once in Royal or Oh Come All Ye.

Such thoughts filled me with sad confusion, particularly when I was near the railway station, gazing at the social solvent high rise that might have looked acceptable in, say, Mile End. Here, it stood out too much, a vertical slum with no covering rookeries. In contrast was the horizontal fiasco of the Dreamland project and the wrecked wooden roller coaster, a Grade II Listed structure apparently. The resort was closed for the season, as far as I could tell it had been all summer. I mean, what kind of seaside place turns its lido into a fucking car park? Just about said it all, I thought, as I joined the asylum seekers, rooted local youth and pensioners in a futile search for something to do. The half-term hip-hop workshop was clearly not for me but I'd missed it in any case. And lovely though the coastal walks were, I needed some structure and some income.

One, if not the other, could be found by doing something that I hadn't done for years: visiting the social. Even during my last stints without work, it quite simply had not been worth the hassle to do this, but rents here, even for the crawling bedsit at Cleveland Court that I now called home, were pricey. Lots of claimants and no private competition meant that landlords had the grip, so rents were jacked to social levels and places kept in disrepair. Refugees, shifted up the coast from Dover, filled the crumbling ruins in the centre, while what money there was cantered gently to the edges. The dole office, job centre, Work Scheme Plus, feckless work-shy pittance project – whatever it was called – reminded me strongly of the Post Office on the Walworth Road, but lacked the community spirit of SE17.

I was assigned a surprisingly cheerful case worker. He was one of those skinny blokes who, late in life, embraces the fat man within, but whose fashion sense remains rooted elsewhere. He wore tight drainpipes, skinny jackets that bulged everywhere and (to my real surprise as he must have been over fifty) Doc Martin boots. Looking at them, I said.

'I don't think I've seen a pair of Docs in over a decade.'

He smiled. 'Old habits, and I do a lot of walking here. And fishing, come to that. Do you fish?'

I shook my head, but he was busying himself with my form.

'Ah, a transpontine. What on earth brings you here? Not the balmy climate, surely?'

I explained as best I could what had occurred, and picked him up on the bridge reference.

'I take it you're from the north then?'

'Eh? Well, 'from' is a bit strong. Lincolnshire originally, but yes, when in London I was a Middlesexer. Moved here to Margate in the early nineties with my partner Alicia, got out of Camden at the right time, I think. Horrible mess the High Street is now, I hear.'

The conversation seemed to send him off into the past, to a time when, he told me, he and Alicia, who was now retired, had both worked for Camden council. He seemed genuinely concerned about my situation and promised to take a personal interest in my case. I was touched – although perhaps that's what they all said nowadays. Maybe they'd been sent on so many empathy courses, no 'client' (odd word in this context) could tell if they were faking it or not.

At my next appointment, Brian, note use of first name, was even more solicitous and told me that he and Alicia wanted to invite me to Christmas dinner at their place. I was flattered, if a bit bemused, and said I'd get back to him.

It turned out that I was back in front of him much sooner than I'd expected. Due to an error in my payments that meant that, but for my savings, I'd have been on the street for Christmas. Fortunately, an offer of a week's work serving dinner to groups of pensioners at one of town's still functioning hotels came up. Brian didn't seem too put out that I would miss their festive meal but suggested I pop round for drinks after work on Christmas Day. The truth was that I'd half intended to do that but found myself, after a series of long shifts, drinking vodka with a couple of young Polish girls working at the hotel.

The waiting work lasted longer than expected and it was some time into the New Year before I next saw Brian, looking very plump and healthy and, despite the shocking weather, carrying his fishing rods and a small sack of bait. He looked so radiant I thought he might have been away somewhere.

'Have a good Christmas?'

'Yes. Yes. Very fulfilling, thank you. Pity you couldn't make it over, but another time eh?'

'You seem pleased. Santa bring you everything you wanted?'

He laughed at this and said, 'Santa and his magic sack rarely let me down. I got some really tasty presents. Now, mustn't keep the hungry fish waiting.' And off he went.

GETTING A TASTE FOR IT

I t had been twenty-five years since Alicia and Brian met, although it was some time after that they started stepping out together. A staffing crisis in the borough's social security office had sent Brian south to St Giles on the edge of Soho. Even though they were part of the same organisation, there was a palpable difference between the staff Brian was used to and the suaver Denmark Street workers. The men sported sophisticated haircuts and the women's shoes were of an altogether higher status than the DMs favoured by his colleagues in Kentish Town. They even walked differently – not quite catwalk, but certainly with a haughtiness that made Brian feel, once again, like a provincial arriving in the city for the first time.

Alicia was the first person Brian remembered meeting. Her hair was feathered into a post-punk quiff, gothic flourishes were already appearing on her bright clothes and those beautiful boots from Red or Dead must have cost a month's wages. A man called Neil Dennison took Brian around and it was almost as if he sensed Brian's fears, because he was terribly supportive and stressed how quickly Brian would get used to it there. Neil's clothing also reassured Brian because, unlike that of his colleagues, it was much more North Camden Comfortable than St Giles Sophisticate.

Brian was completely in awe of Alicia and her colleagues, who spoke of pubs, clubs and shebeens (Taboo, Blitz) that he had never heard of. Before then, he'd secretly rather prided himself on his

Soho knowledge and in Kentish Town had been something of an authority with his Time Out data and City Limits wisdom. Back in dependable Kentish Town a month or so later, he found himself reversing roles and escorting Neil, who found it a good deal easier there than Brian had in the West End, about.

In the aftermath of Neil's arrest, Brian and Alicia really got to know each other amid the flying memos, heartfelt discussions, group hugs, plenaries, sessions, meetings (ordinary and extraordinary) and offers of help. All the staff who had ever worked with Neil, all the staff who had ever worked in Camden job centres, and their relatives, had been offered counselling. Under the circumstances, it wasn't surprising that people got together, kept the situation in-house and huddled around their shared trauma. There was, of course, the shock of finding out that a work colleague had been one of Britain's top serial killers. But beyond that, there was the issue of the meat pies.

It had been a tradition at staff functions and special occasions for workers to bring a dish and some booze. For most people, this entailed a swift trip to Tesco's for sausage rolls and crisps, but the more culinary creative brought in home-made fancies, cakes and, in Neil's case, very tasty meat pies. One obvious result of the revelations after his arrest was that the percentage of vegetarians among the Camden council workforce, already higher than the national average, hit eighty per cent in some departments. There were staff-rooms in which all meat was banned and the mutton-eating minority had to scoff their bacon sarnies in pariahical corners, away from the vision of the vegan vigilantes. Even those who had been vegetarian all through the trade pie years, as they were referred to, were not particularly smug. This was because their partners, or at least, people they'd snogged on the nights in question (few Christmas dos are as bacchanalian as a job centre jamboree) were carnivores.

Among this general fright and the calculating of how much people had eaten and what were the odds that any of the dishes had actually been fricassee of rent boy, Brian and Alicia found themselves oddly apart from the others. They were not particularly affected by the panic or worried by the possibilities. 'Bit of a fuss about not much,' Brian had told one counsellor, who had advised him not to repeat this to his colleagues. He had only done so once and, luckily, it was to Alicia, who concurred and added that there wasn't much that could be done about it now, because whatever it was had long passed out of their systems and graduated the finishing stool of the sewage works. By now, in all probability, it was so thoroughly decomposed that the same molecules had probably re-entered the food chain as organic carrot.

Brian was amused by this refreshing outlook. He also found something exciting about this powerful (she had risen to area manager), slightly older, outspoken woman. They had both changed since their first meeting and, although Brian was still overawed, he could now at least talk to her and look at her at the same time. For Alicia's part, she always enjoyed being looked at and talked to by an obviously interested and sympathetic younger man.

These early meetings after group seminars and training courses led to drinks after work, cinema trips, walks at weekends, dancing and sex; though not necessarily in that order. Alicia had decided to have Brian the day of the first crisis meeting. The events and all that talk of firm meat acted as an aphrodisiac for her. And she hadn't failed to spot the cool thrill in Brian's voice, in contrast to the appalled tones of their other workmates.

One of the advantages of being in a senior position and having a relatively lengthy record of work in the same place is an unbeatable knowledge of which rooms are likely to be unoccupied at any given time. So it was that Alicia fucked Brian roughly over the desk of the Chief Sanitation Engineer, making sure that when she'd finished riding him he knelt in front of her to clean up her pipes. It was a few weeks later that they had their next assignation. Alicia organised for Brian to be kept late at his office in Theobalds Road when she arrived in a long Mac with nothing underneath but her underwear, and with some handcuffs in her pocket. 'I've come to make a claim,' she had begun. After that, their sessions became more regular, Alicia demanding both regular and emergency appointments.

After several years of living together they were able to take advantage of a shake up in both London local government and housing. Camden Council, in a bid to solve its housing crisis, was bribing people to move out of the area by offering them cash and a bigger home. So it was that Alicia was able to swap her one-bedroom flat on the crumbling Somers Town Estate for a three-bedroom detached property on the coast near Margate, and to wrangle positions in Kent Social Services for both Brian and herself.

Life was duller than it had been in London but the spare bedrooms and the greater space allowed them to entertain at home more, and Kent was full of can-accommodate, bi-curious couples. The temptations were greater too. In the extreme Goth clubs they'd begun to frequent in London, they could indulge, even in the AIDS years, something of their passion for human flesh by biting or drinking the blood of a surprisingly large number of volunteers. It was Brian who had first proposed Operation Homeless Feed, but Alicia who perfected it and carried it to its logical extreme.

'No one likes to be alone at Christmas.'

'No one is meant to be.'

'It's the peak time for suicides.'

'People often make a new start afterwards, in the new year. Or go back to the family home.'

'Let's check the records to see who might do.'

So, in the month before Christmas, they would trawl the list of claimants to find people who weren't from the area, were unlikely to be missed and, crucially, were homeless at the right time. If need be, this could be precipitated by a judicious withholding of a housing cheque, resulting in a perfectly timed eviction. Where else would the claimant run but the social, where Alicia or Brian would reel them in with an offer of accommodation over the festive period. Not all of them ended up in the pot, but a good many did; and the couple had learned from Neil's disposal mistakes. This meant that Brian made a great many fishing trips with his special bait every January. He never even minded if some fish got away, for he knew that someone out there would be eating what he had put back into the food chain.

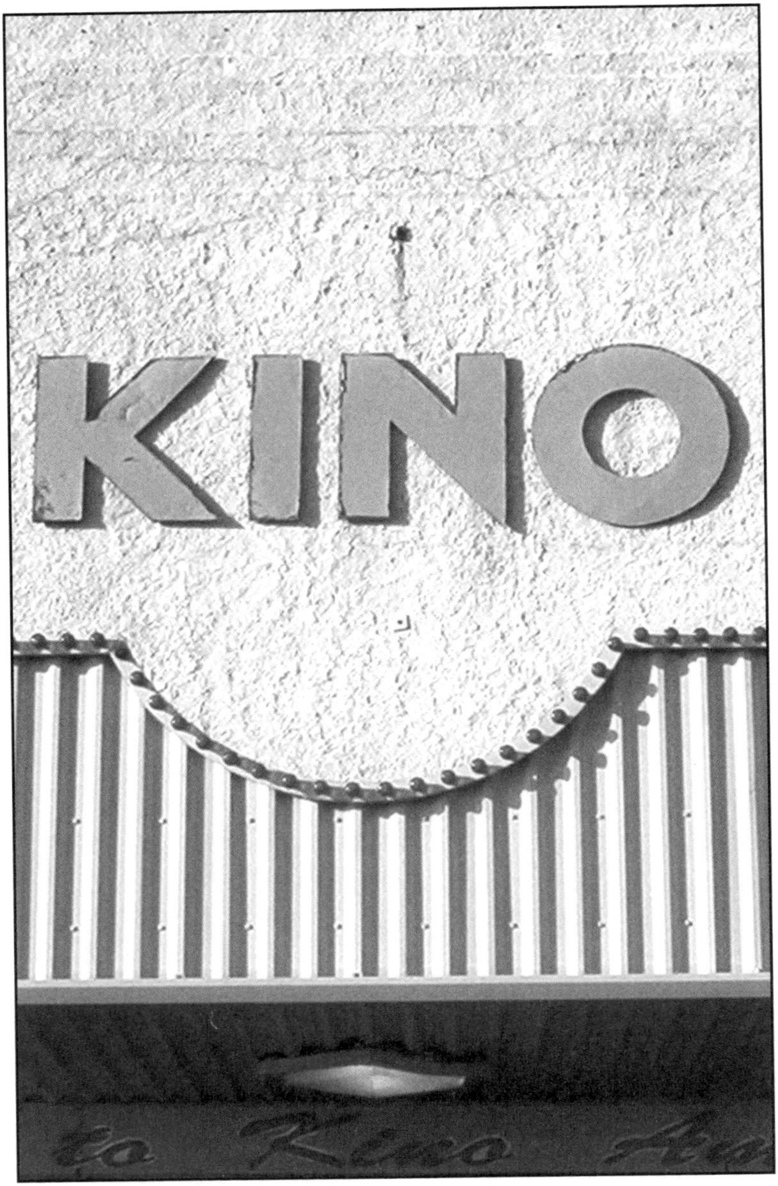
KINO

THE END OF THE LINE

AFTER NEARLY A YEAR IN GREAT YARMOUTH I CAME TO WHAT I felt was the end of the line. In a sense, all my stopping places had been that, but in Walton I just felt it more. This was less to do with the place itself than my own condition. I'd always travelled alone, by my own methods and therefore, after a fashion, had always been master of my time. In Walton, I was juveniled by a lack of adequate transport. To many who lived in the heart of a major city, driving was at best a luxury and at worst an unnecessary imposition, and I was one of those who had never learned. My spatial awareness was that of a cyclist anyway, so I'd probably have been a menace behind the wheel. I could have cycled to where I worked at Harwich, but the weather and time were against it – even though the docks were clearly visible across the estuary, the route was miles by land. So I accepted the offer of a lift from a neighbour, Nick. Although it was peculiar to be dependent in this way, I appreciated the company and Nick had some great local stories to tell, which was just as well because his car radio was broken.

Yarmouth had felt increasingly oppressive, like a place under siege, so Walton came as a relief. The walks were far more interesting, along the Naze or swinging to Frinton. But even here, on the edge of land, on a back route of a back route of the line from Liverpool Street, I couldn't escape the dim beat of the city by the Thames. On the fringes of Walton was Beaumont Quay, where a tablet recorded the fact that the quay had been constructed from stones recycled from Old London Bridge. Nearby was another refugee from the Great Wen, The Rose, an old Thames sailing barge that was now just a skeleton of mud-pickled ribs. Another quay was the site of a smuggler's pub that had been converted into a home in Edwardian times by society photographer Nigel Henderson. He was clearly a man with great powers of persuasion, as he'd managed to bring the Bloomsbury Set to Walton. This was a concept I found very difficult to take and idly wondered whom I might bring down here and whether my team would come.

I doubted it. What could it have offered them, and what could I have given them? Two years had disappeared since I'd left, and my friends were no wiser about my motives for doing so. Or at least, I was no more willing to expose them. We all had our secrets, and I supposed their importance could be gauged by how far people would go to protect them.

On one of our journeys to work, Nick told me about possibly the strangest link of all between Walton on Naze and the big smoke. We had driven past a place called Gull Cottage, once home to William Withey Gull. The son of an Essex bargeman, Gull cured the Prince of Wales of typhoid and subsequently became Queen Victoria's personal physician. It was alleged that he had been the man who roamed London's streets and cut up a number of women, to protect the reputation of Queen Victoria's grandson, Prince 'Eddy', Duke of Clarence. It was certainly William Gull, in his capacity as court physician, who signed the certificate to put east end prostitute Annie Crook away. The poor girl was confined to hospitals and workhouses until she eventually died, insane. A similar fate befell Gull himself, who was incarcerated in an asylum under the name of 'Mason', while a sham death and burial was staged, with a coffin filled with stones. There was speculation – well, Nick conjectured, anyway – that Gull might not be alone in his real grave at Thorpe Le Soken, and that the tomb actually contained three people. The last loose ends of the Ripper case buried out east like so much landfill.

It was another burial that preoccupied me when Nick dropped me off one evening, a few months into my Walton stay. After picking up a fish supper I ambled back past the pier, appraising a rare, and upsetting, message from Sally, whom I had entrusted with my e-mail address. She was an infrequent correspondent but I'd promised her that I'd keep this line of communication open in case of emergencies. Now, one had occurred. Omar was dead. Sally understood that it had been some sort of stroke or a blood clot on the brain. His funeral was to be held near Stratford on Thursday, in three days' time. Handy, I thought, for me. Straight there if you took the right approach train. No mucking about going in and out of Liverpool Street.

I was trying to picture Omar and attempting to imagine how Poppy must be feeling, when I got another jolt from the past, this time visual. I caught sight of a woman, pushing a child along the seafront. A beautiful woman – fit and muscular with auburn hair and a sort of dreamy way of moving. Her background was hard to place but what most grabbed the attention were her eyes, which had an aquatic quality. I knew her from somewhere. She looked up as I passed, a glimmer of recognition in those eyes. Jenny, I thought. Jenny Gite from Brockwell Lido.

That was nothing to the shock I got the following night.

I'd been seeing Ruby, a local girl not quite out of her twenties. I couldn't understand why she still lived in Walton. She worked, in some administrative capacity, for the University at Colchester, and had never taken that extra step and stayed on the train to London, as so many others did. She'd gone to Ipswich for her education, and had only worked in Manningtree before Colchester. She fell awkwardly between those who had the push to go, and those who stayed to push prams. That much I could see, but why she fell for me was less clear. Perhaps she recognised something in me – the attraction and repulsion of the shimmering western glow, perhaps, or the shared uncertainty of purpose. Or maybe she just wanted someone she could look after a bit, to take her mind off her own failings.

Outlining the last of these possibilities in the pub after work that Tuesday night might not have been the brightest thing I'd ever done, though in my defence, I did have a lot of other things on my mind. I told her I was going to a funeral and I think that she was initially hurt by my failure to explicitly ask her to go with me. In truth, I wasn't sure whether I wanted her along or not. This was a family affair, after all; outsiders would always be exactly that – outside. They were days of reckoning for more than just the departed, a bonding time for those who were close, and I knew just how impatient Lucy, let alone Sally, would be towards some insignificant other, moping on the fringes.

I didn't put it quite like that but my reasoning was that some things were better not left unsaid, otherwise Ruby could have made worse assumptions. I gazed after her as she retreated from the Victory, where we had been sitting in the restaurant, apart from the main bar, until her departing figure was blotted out by a rangy blonde man.

'They all abandon you in the end, don't they Carl?', came a familiar voice. 'Or do you just pre-empt them by leaving them first?'

I looked up and stared.

It wasn't the face of Martin that I'd last seen – blotched and decayed, enfeebled with drugs and half bald with the conflicting demands of disease and cure. This was the Martin of years before that; upright, sharp featured, brown hair swept up into something approaching a quiff but fiercely barbered along the sides. He was wearing dark jeans and a t-shirt mostly covered by a wheat yellow

cashmere cardigan. The corner of his upturned mouth held a cigarette like Popeye clutched his pipe. He withdrew the tab, saying,
'Thinking of my future always makes me want to smoke,' before
grinding the butt into the pub floor with his winkle-pickers. An
odd choice of shoe, perhaps, for a town built on the shellfish trade.
Then, looking directly at me, he asked, 'What's occurring? You look
like you've seen a ghost.'

Martin sat down, muttering that, under the circumstances,
it might be some time before he was invited to do so and, once
settled, he looked across at me, grinned and said, 'Jenny thought
she saw you on the waterfront yesterday. Not hard to track you
down in a place like this. Incidentally,' he added, looking out at
the street down which Ruby had left. 'Your girl. She doesn't like
horses, does she?'

Shocked at seeing Martin, I was bewildered further by the
peculiarity of the question and found myself saying, 'No, no, she's
scared of them. Something in her childhood...'

He seemed amused by this and added enigmatically 'That's good
for her, then. Very good for her. How did you meet her? Through
the personals? Shy country type seeks older Metropolitan? Prim
Rose seeks Dull Stan. Must have geseaux?' Martin paused, shifted
direction. 'But what about you? What happened to you, eh? What
became of the people?' He laughed. 'Still in contact with the old
firm?' He looked me up and down and said, 'No, I guess you're not.
Not even lovely Lucy? Or Sally?' He must have caught some flick-
er in my face, because he said, 'Ah! I thought, maybe. The tie that
binds. Or is it the binds that tie?'

I didn't react to this, but said coldly, 'For a dead man, you seem
in remarkably rude health.'

'I like that. Though it's illness, not health that's usually rude, isn't it? All those burps, farts, emissions and seepings.' He stopped and lit another cigarette. 'Funny things, funerals. I'd have loved to have been at my own but you can't have everything, can you?' he said, expansively. 'It's why I'm down here, as it happens, for a funeral. Jenny, too, and Walter, though I'm not sure you ever knew Walter, did you?'

'The blonde guy?' I guessed.

'Yeah. Used to study at Chelsea. Extraordinary fellow. Hung like a horse. Not that you'd be interested in that.' He blew his smoke at the ceiling.

'One of my stranger friends, though by no means the oddest. Well, aren't you surprised to see me?' He sounded offended. 'I mean, you never believed in ghosts before, you don't have to start now.' He held out his arm. 'Look, feel, solid. Made from the stuff of angels!'

There was no denying that this apparition was flesh and blood and simply too Martin to be an impostor, however good a facsimile might be made with surgery. After this, there was only one obvious question. 'If you're alive,' I said, 'then who did I murder?'

'I think you'll find it's "whom" did I murder.' Martin scratched his head and smiled wider, before catching the look on my face and holding up his hands. 'Whichever, I guess it's a fair question. Do you remember Phillip? I suppose, in a way, you killed him. But then again, Phillip wasn't really Phillip any more, so I'm not sure it's true to say it was really Phillip you killed. Look, let me get a round in and I'll explain.'

I sat, mute, while he swept off to the bar. I could hear the land-lady's gruff laughter, rusty with disuse, as Martin handed her the money. I'd only heard her make that sound once before, when a reg-ular had brought the news that her ex-husband had been gored by a bull in Spain. It was clear that Martin had lost none of his charm or, as Sally had sniffily referred to it, his common touch.

He returned with two pints of Shepherds Neame and a brace of large whiskies.

'Grouse do you, will it? I remembered the ice.' He settled in his chair, raised his glass and said, 'Here's looking at you.'

'Mud in your eye,' I replied. Then I said, 'So, can we proceed on the assumption that I am neither dead nor hallucinating, nor otherwise in some kind of parallel dimension.'

He laughed. 'Those are always good premises to begin from.'

'With that as a starting point,' I said, 'am I to assume that you are actually Martin? Or are you some sort of – how did you refer to Phillip again? – a sort of not-Martin with the essence of Martin?'

'Very good. Essence of Martin! Not sure that would ever be a market leader but weirder things have happened.'

'They certainly have,' I agreed. 'So perhaps you can explain what's been going on and whether I should be worried about some kind of punishment, from the lily law or some supernatural Sweeney.'

Martin laughed, really roared, in his infectious fashion. 'Lily law! How dolly! But nanti polari! And no sharpis are after you in this world or any other, as far as I am aware.'

'Good. That information comes as a considerable relief.' Though I caught something in his expression that suggested it might not be the police I needed to fear.

He hooted again, and said, 'Do you know, I have missed you and your gift for understatement, rather more than I care to admit. I've been coming across a lot of incredibly po-faced people of late.' He took a huge swig of his bitter and continued, 'So, the story, soup to blow job, yes?'

'The full twelve Reals, please.'

'Well, I suppose you could say it all started with Phillip, late of

Shepherds Bush and currently residing in a secure unit in the sub-
urbs near Monks Orchard Road. Except that the Phillip in Bedlam
is not the real Phillip. The real Phillip, I'm afraid, was assassinated
by your own hand.' Martin looked at my fingers, battered by their
heavy work on the docks, before continuing. 'Now, do you remember that, prior to his incarceration, Phillip was behaving very oddly
indeed?'

'All that raving about time travel and sleeping with historical
figures, you mean? You're about to tell me that's all true, aren't you?'

Martin nodded. 'Afraid so but Phillip was no longer Phillip.
The person you thought was Phillip had been taken over by an
earthbound angel. It had swapped places with him. I won't bore you
with the details but it's a rare procedure.' He took his cardy off and
looked around the bar. No one was anywhere near us, so he went
on. 'Now, this entity had an intense desire for mortality, but also a
rather idealised, romantic if you will, view of the human condition.
After a year or so of being Phillip, it got bored. Mind you, in all
honesty, would any of us have lasted even that long as Phillip?'

I laughed and had to agree. 'Two months I think would do me.'

'Exactly. So what does this hitherto immortal being do? It tries
to find a way back, but learns, horribly, that there's no possibility of
that happening. It has crossed a bridge it can cross only once in that
particular direction. So this is the moment when the earthbound
angel – the being formerly known as Phillip – goes nuts.' Martin
paused to let a couple get past us. 'Now, you know what I'm like.
By this time I know that I'm going to die, so I'm starting to panic.
I'm also very interested in what is being said about immortality, so
I question further and it all comes out. A whole eternity of this
being's life, and something else as well.'

He stopped and pointed to the gents. 'Gotta go. Even angels

have to pee, you know, there are some laws of nature that must be obeyed. Get another round in, will you?'

The landlady had returned to her normal crabby self in time to serve me, and when I got back to the table Martin had sparked up another smoke and was exhaling luxuriantly. 'Not long left for this, eh? They'll be banning beer as well eventually, you know.'

'I see prophecy comes with the package then,' I said. 'Can I have one of those? I might as well join in the last days of smoking.'

'Good on you,' he said, pocketing the lighter after sparking my red. 'So yes, the package deal. Although the creature formerly... shall we just call him 'Phil'?' I nodded. 'So, 'Phil' couldn't go back to his immortal form. But he had found a way for other people to do it, thereby at least getting revenge on the real Phillip, who was now enjoying his new immortal state. I was the only person 'Phil' trusted, the only one he'd told about all this. I was sympathetic to him and I had motivation. I was dying.' He put his cigarette out.

I looked across at him and said, 'So, to summarise, 'Phil' tells you how to become the sort of immortal creature he had been, by swapping identities with Phillip, but it meant returning Phillip to mortality in the process?'

'In one,' Martin nodded. 'Except that, because it was me, mortality was a limited concept. I left it as long as possible, waited until I was very ill indeed. I wanted to give Philip as decent an innings as I could. But I had everything set up for my salvation. I'd briefed you to administer the morphine if 'I' started raving and lost my mind and, of course, that is exactly what happened when I swapped places with Phillip and he became me. He totally and absolutely broke down.' Martin glanced at me, sensing disapproval. 'Look, it was him or me. I'm sorry. I like my friends, really I do, but life is life and mine was ending.'

'Well, I actually ended it, didn't I?' I gulped my drink. 'That phrase, "I could swing for you". I could, in both meanings, right now!'

Martin laughed. 'Okay, fair point, but I was desperate. You of all people know what it was like for me at the end.'

We stared at each other a while, then he said, 'I'll spare you the details, but the ceremony involved is a form of sex magic. As opposed to magic sex. Now, normally, the sexual vampire, which is what 'Phil' was, chooses their victim, grabs some DNA, and that person's identity, for a while, then carries on. No harm done, and the victim just remembers a particularly vivid wet dream.' He swallowed the whisky in one.

'I wasn't that happy about having sex with Phillip. Mind you, not as distressed as he was. You see, 'Phil' had figured out a foolproof method of luring any sexual vampire, including Phillip, that involved making it impossible for them not to select whoever activates the bait. Phil had also sussed out a way to reverse the process that transforms an incubus into a mortal. That's what he taught me, and that's what I did, and that's why I'm here.' He finished this and his pint at the same time, and slammed down the glass.

I was stunned but managed to ask, 'You still haven't said why you're here. In Walton, I mean.'

'Neither have you. What are running from?' He paused, not really expecting an answer, so went on, 'For me, it's all down to Jenny. She's not exactly what she seems. You see, in my new guise I've got access to things I couldn't have dreamed about before.' He rearranged the table, glanced over his shoulder and leaned closer. 'One of the things I've discovered is that there really are such things as mermaids.'

I coughed at this, not wishing to appear impolite or over-credu-

lous, and said, 'And you're about to tell me that Jenny Gite, late of
Brockwell Park Lido, is one of them? Well, she was a swift one in
the pool but I don't remember seeing any fins and I think word
might have reached me if anyone else had.'

'It doesn't work like that, Martin said. 'She's not fish all the
time, just sometimes. Like a werewolf at the full moon. Anyway,
she's down here for a relative's funeral and as far as I'm aware, no
man has ever seen a mermaid's funeral. At least, they haven't seen
one and lived. I, of course, no longer quite fit the category of 'man'.
But you do, I think, so… if you're interested?' He laughed as he said
this, but I caught a kind of probing intensity in his gaze. He wanted
me to come, needed me even, in some way. I was sure of it. Bizarrely,
I was reminded of our early days in London, before he knew many
people, when he used to beg Sally, Femi or myself (depending on
the venue) to accompany him to some new and fruity club.

He stood up to leave.

'Meet me at the Kino amusements tomorrow at seven, if you
fancy it. I can fill you in on the way. Now though, I really must fly.'
With that, he was out of the door.

LAST RITES

Carl had drunk quite a lot that night and had spent most of the time worrying about his sanity. He believed Martin was real. He'd even found a way of verifying Martin's presence with the landlady. As to the stuff about mermaids, well, if Martin was telling the truth about himself, why not about that too? And what the hell had he meant about Ruby and horses?

Having doused his doubts with Scotch, Carl eventually slept. The next day, he was keen to dismiss the whole encounter as a particularly long and bizarre hallucination but nevertheless went to the library straight after work.

Carl's hand hovered over the mouse as the curser drifted above the 'send' icon. He thought how much harder emails were to dispatch than letters. He'd spent ages on this one, not just telling the story – that had been easy enough – but also getting the tone right. He wanted Sally to know that he'd met Martin, to realise where he was and a bit of what was going on but he didn't want her down there, not just yet. Besides that, he wished to go Omar's funeral but was haunted by the thought that it might not be possible for him to do that. A part of him wondered if these were his last words to Sally and how much difference that made. Did it really make any? After all, his parting words to Steve at work had probably been, 'See you tomorrow, then'. And to Lucy, 'Don't forget to put ice in mine'. Was he really going to improve on that? Did it help anyone, in the end?

As so often happened – too often, he reflected bitterly – the decision ended up being made by someone else. A man coughed behind him and he involuntarily clicked the mouse. Too late now, Carl thought, no recall on these, it's gone. He glanced round the library. It was already nearly dark and it looked as if the staff were dying to go home, despite the cosy intimacy of the building. It stood adjacent to the car park where, on Mondays, travelling jesters in strange clothes entertained the locals with exotic goods and peculiar sales pitches. As he strolled down to the converted cinema, Carl doubted whether they could compare to the mysterious sights in store for him later that evening.

Martin – and Carl supposed he must call him that – was very much his old self, full of the absurdities and potential that life offered. He was standing outside the arcade by a plastic representation of a horse that really wasn't at all right in terms of scale, colouring or expression. He was wearing a beautiful dark coat, cashmere and wool mix by the look of it, and had a hat cocked back on his head. He was staring across the road and out to sea at the lights of the ships on the horizon.

'Trains and boats and planes,' he half sang, at Carl's approach. 'I keep trying to work out which one is Sealand, the independent republic. Must be nice to own your own country, even if it is just an old gun emplacement. How are you? Did you bother getting in touch with Sally?'

Carl was about to ask how he knew he'd emailed her, but there was no need for a supernatural explanation there – it was obvious that he would have at least thought about it. 'Oh, well. Omar's funeral, you know,' he muttered.

'Won't be anything like tonight's, I can assure you,' Martin said. 'You never really knew all my more unusual acquaintances, and let me tell you they've got weirder in the past few years. The opportunities this new life affords, the opportunities in worlds you cannot imagine...'

He carried on as they started to walk along the promenade, 'I started even before I got sick, I think. Walter was the first, but even before him I'd been delving into the stranger side of London life. You wouldn't believe what's just below the surface, passing as normal. You just have to know where to look and be brave enough to follow through.'

Carl could remember Martin going to meetings across London and regaling him with the stories he brought back, usually just snatches of conversation. 'Our coven are having an open evening on Thursday, clothes optional,' he'd quote. Or, 'So, the goddess was standing in my living room.' This, Carl realised, had been public face paganism; normal people who liked unusual things, good people whose religiosity took them down a different path. Martin had reckoned that you could happily spend four nights a week at one or other such meetings without getting at all involved, and certainly without any danger of finding yourself crucified upside down and naked on Blackheath. The trouble, he contended, was that really, that sort of thing was exactly what he was interested in. It seemed that he'd found it after a while; those were the stories he didn't report.

They reached the beach huts, and it transpired that Martin had been camping out in one of them. 'Surprisingly comfortable in a way,' he said, before suggesting taking the seaside route rather than the more leisurely road past the houses to the Tower.

Looking out over the sands, Martin said, 'Gives you a sense of passing time, doesn't it? The beach out there is the exposed floor of the Jurassic sea throwing up the fossilised remains of creatures that lived when your ancestors were in the trees, or even before then. It's a great stretch of eternity beyond the grasp of the minds of men. I'm not even sure whether my kind would have been around.' He paused awhile and said, 'Carl, remember watching Wings of Desire? That great bit where the angels are talking about the coming of man and how happy they were because now, for the first time, they'd have language? It must have been like that for my breed too, waiting for evolution finally to throw up a species worth shagging. Incredible. No wonder they were gagging for it when Homo sapiens finally popped up!'

Martin laughed at his own joke, then said, 'I could stand here for aeons and watch the revelation of the past and the shifting of the future.'

Carl coughed, which seemed to break Martin's reverie, and they began the ascent to the Tower. Carl wanted to know whether anyone knew what was planned for the night. Martin smiled.

'Any locals, you mean? I doubt it. There are watchers in the bushes, in the battered gun emplacements, in case anyone comes too close. The older natives stay clear on certain evenings. It's like a race memory with them.' Martin stopped to look around. 'Apparently, during the war, there was a lot of bother with this area being so heavily militarised – troops everywhere. And they heeded their officers, not local gossip. It meant that some poor sod from Lancaster or somewhere would end up having to be killed. Of course, their bodies were never found and the odd sapper going AWOL during a time of mass slaughter, well, it's unlikely to raise much of a fuss, is it? I guess that's how legends start, then people just pass them on. I remember you telling me about the American nuclear authorities spreading tales of a cursed Indian burial ground right where they wanted to dump spent fuel. They figured that stories last longer than fences. Maybe they're right.'

Martin drew heavily on a cigarette he'd just lit ('One plus

eh? No cancer to worry about!') and talked all the way up the hill towards the Tower on top of the Naze by the Tower.

'All man-made things corrode. How long do reckon this has, what with global warming and coastal erosion?' Martin caressed the brickwork. 'I love a nice cup of tea. Did you know this was a tea-room in the 1770s? Tea had a racier reputation then, and the rich folk held orgies in the top floors. Lord Sandwich – he of the butty fame – brought parties of actresses here. At one party in the spring of 1779, a character called Reverend Hackman fell hard for one of the actresses, a Ms Martha Ray, and followed her to London. He waited for her to come out of Covent Garden Theatre and shot her in the temple, just for rejecting him. The tea rooms were closed for 225 years after that, but then, that's just a blink in the greater scheme of things isn't it?'

It's like turning on a tap, Carl thought. He could also tell that immortality was growing on Martin. With the realisation came a sense of his own insignificance, and Carl imagined himself as a small flickering flame that he feared might soon be extinguished. As the pair headed towards the tip of the Naze, where the woodland got thicker and the paths less distinct, Carl was aware of creatures stir-ring in the bushes. He knew that mount jack deer and rabbits were common here, but he didn't think these sounds were being caused by the shy, skittish activities of those creatures. There was a stealthy deliberateness to the movements that unsettled him.

Martin talked on, about debt and balance, he spoke of different orders and manners that in some cases predated, and in others grew up alongside, the human. He nattered about price of admission and honour systems, and appeared to be building up to something he was unsure of how to get to. It all sounded a bit abstract to Carl until Martin finally said,

'The merpeople have been here for centuries, you know. As long as anyone can remember, this site has been special to them. One of them was caught in the 12th century, up the coast at Orford, and was held in a castle for six months before escaping back into the ocean. He never talked. Also, there have been sightings at Dunwich and green children at Woolpit. Still. That's pretty good going, three times in a thousand years. I could never be so discreet.'

He looked around them and whispered, 'The ones round here are more bloodthirsty than elsewhere, and that was exacerbated during the last war. You see, contrary to received history, the Germans did try to invade the mainland once, but Churchill had a secret weapon.' He paused as if listening for something. 'This weapon was a thin film of flammable liquid on the sea and beaches, and it was ignited when the Nazi boats started to land the troops. It was horrible. Whole sections of the coast up in flames, and naturally that didn't do a lot for marine wildlife.'

Martin's face hardened a bit. 'Greenpeace would never allow that sort of thing today,' he joked. 'Some of the German survivors, charred and broken, spoke of beings that had been alongside them in the water, creatures neither fully human nor completely fish that snatched some of their comrades. Naturally the British dismissed these reports as the deranged ravings of dying men.'

They were walking in the open now, water on three sides of them and the moon up. Carl was happy to be out of the trees. Martin lit another cigarette and returned to the war story.

'The merpeople weren't rescuing the soldiers, of course. They were taking them as tribute. You see, they believe that, whenever one of them passes over into the pools of eternity, they must take a human slave with them as payment so they can enter Dreitchell, as they call it. It can't be just any human, either. It has to be someone with blood on their hands. Soldiers are likely to fit the criteria, as, obviously, does a murderer. Funny thing is, they can smell it on a person. You, of course, reek of it.'

Martin put out his smoke and looked apologetically at Carl. 'I'm sorry, mate, but you had no chance from the moment Jenny saw you on the waterfront. They were getting desperate before you turned up. I mean, you'd think Essex would be full of killers wouldn't you? But they were genuinely scared that the deceased would have no payment for the awful gods of the gateway. The alternative – mermaid hell, if you will – is to be consigned to a desert for eternity. They wouldn't let that happen.'

Carl took the cigarette Martin offered him. He had known there was danger, he had known that the real Martin (let alone the part-demon one in front of him) could never be entirely trusted. Perhaps he had even expected something like this. Martin's words had been, 'No man has ever seen a mermaid's funeral and lived'. He always did promise an exciting night out, though. Made you feel that anyone else would be dying for the chance to go. Well, here he was. Literally dying for it.

'Same old Martin, eh?' Carl said angrily. 'Finding a use, old friends for new, is it? I'm not sure I like being someone's ticket of entry. Theirs to fucking water world paradise, and your voucher to this! I should sell the lot of them to Captain Bird's Eye. Not sure what can be done with you, though. So where is fucking Nemo? When am I going to get the pleasure of meeting the scaly chops?'

Martin shook his head and said, 'It's not like you to be prejudiced, Carl. They like to be known as "people of aquatic heritage" or, in the US, "aquatic Americans".'

'I think you might show a little less tolerance if you were going to be… what? Eaten by something you'd normally find wrapped up in small pieces of rice on a conveyer belt?'

Martin howled with laughter. 'There you go again, that under-statement. I really will miss it. But then again, I don't have to, do I?' His eyes narrowed, more in expectation than hostility. Collecting himself, he said. 'Look. You were a dead man. By the way, you know how they refer to death? They say the person "walks with the apes"! Good, eh?' He took out a hip flask, drank from it then offered it to Carl.

'As I said, you were a corpse from the time Jenny spotted you and smelled your crime.'

'My so-called crime was helping you to a more comfortable ending.'

'Which is why they allowed me to bring you here, Carl, because I asked them to. I thought you'd be alive a bit longer that way, and we could spend some quality time together. I know I wasn't exactly the best company in those days in my sick room. There is something else as well.'

Carl handed back the flask, which Martin pocketed, and waited for him to continue.

'You see, I learned something else from 'Phil': that the ability to live as a human has its pluses. He realised how important friend-ship was. And long-term relationships. I miss my friends, you know, I miss them terribly, but I can't appear to them, can I? Not as a dead man. But you could. Even if you were deceased, I mean, because they wouldn't know you'd passed on, and there's no reason why they ever would.' Something glittered in Martin's eyes.

Carl looked at Martin for a long time. Finally, he said, 'Greater love has no man, but that he will lay down the life of his friend? I don't think so, do you? I don't think I could be party to deceiving Sally and the others on quite that scale.'

'But they'd still have you,' countered Martin. 'Lucy would still have you. They love you and they'd never know you'd gone.'

Carl shook his head again. 'No, they wouldn't have me, they'd have you, looking like me. And under the current circumstances, I'm not sure of the wisdom of that. Sorry.'

Martin's face communicated a depth of sadness Carl had seldom seen on anyone before. It was the sorrow of ages, the wretchedness of the fallen angels, the anguish of eternity. Much the same look that he'd always given on being refused entry to a club. Carl felt pity, even now, he felt pity, as Martin forced a smile and said,

'Well I can't make you. Anyway, I heard from Sally that you weren't all that of an athlete in the bedroom.'

'She told you that!' Despite everything, Carl was amused and shocked. 'Yeah well. It was a fulfilled dream. I guess they never live up to reality. As I recall, we were completely plastered at the time.'

'Maybe, maybe. So. I suppose my fantasy will go unfulfilled, of seeing all of our friends as you.' Martin held out a hand.

Carl whispered to Martin, 'They're not going to find this easy, you know. I'm going to go down fighting the bastards.'

Martin looked enormously sad for a moment, then smiled and said, 'That's my Carl. You batter a couple of them, eh?'

With that he was off, round a dark corner and into the trees. Carl stood his ground, the glowing ember in his fist, the lights of Harwich ahead of him and death all around.

A SMALL GROUP STOOD HUDDLED ON THE SHORE. WEAK SUNLIGHT from a Simpson's sky tried its best to warm them, but it had used up all its energy burning off the morning mist. A woman with grey-flecked raven hair and wearing a red coat threw a wreath into the waters. She was talking loudly almost ranting at the others, the sea and to the sky.

'He would have thought this appropriate. The wanker. He would have thought it apt to disappear at the point of a disappeared London! This is the spot where the mightier Thames, the one that drained the Welsh mountains, the original Thames before the ice age, before the crack in Goring Gap relocated it south. This is where it once roared into the wilderness out there!' Here she paused and pointed weakly at the horizon. A woman in a smart leather coat and dark beret took her arm but the first shrugged her off. 'Yes this is where London might have been but for a bloody accident of geology a few millennia or so ago. London! He still fucking disappeared in London.' The woman finally sagged, her fury expressed.

Sally had organised everything, of course, with Lucy in a supporting role. There was something of the school roll call about the event. Lucy (present), Poppy (here), Femi (yeah), Sally (um hmm), Robert (present), Melissa (here), Joe (yup) and also, on Femi's arm, Oona. To one side were Graham and Charlotte with their youngster Billy. No Carl though, this time, and of course, no Omar.

They others milled around, telling each other the rest of their do-you-remember-when stories, and Sally stalked the sands, trying to hide her anger. Lucy was playing with Billy. Suddenly, he ran towards a rock pool, by which stood a lovely child, a beautiful girl, maybe two years old, with auburn hair and eyes that Lucy recognised but couldn't place. But then, in her emotional state, everything seemed to trigger some recollection. The girl smiled at Billy, but Billy stopped short and retreated, crying for his mother.

NOTES ON THE STORIES

We there aren't too many of these this time as we have been a bit more urban legend and a bit less folklore than in previous volumes and of course the stories are set all over the place. The Brighton tale owes much to the so called 'yuppie punishment' sub genre of the 1990s but with housing costs being what they are it is almost surprising something similar hasn't happened. There is a however a long history of strange disappearances, UFO sightings and other peculiar events involving Clapham Woods just north of Worthing. It seems some nights you move for goths, cultists and people who still watch the X Files rustling through the undergrowth. The woods are well worth a visit though, particularly in early autumn as that way if you don't find anything spooky you can at least be compensated by a fine selection of fruit, nuts and berries.

It's a shame we couldn't include Hastings with its Crowley associations in our collection of towns but that and our tale of penal colonies in Great Yarmouth had to be axed. The latter though is available online and hopefully answers the tricky question about what happened to the vanquished in the Norwegian troll wars, as well as going some way to explaining why Great Yarmouth isn't quite the full postcode. Margate on the other hand is totally proper with its fabulous shell grotto and Chas and Dave eulogies. Equally it seemed the logical place for a London cannibal to head for, as clearly the council there lost their sense of what it is to be human when they turned the seafront lido into a car park.

All roads lead to Walton. Well not all of them but Walton is interesting because in a parallel universe it really might have been the site of London. Or at least where the Thames estuary would have started for the sea if it hadn't been for the river's change of course during the last ice age. There are also the Metropolitan reminders dotted around the town and anyone who doubts the dangers from aquatic creatures in that part of the world might be well advised to search around the exposed ancient sea bed for fossilized shark's teeth, or indeed mermaid's purses, because they can be quite careless with their belongings.

There are other non supernatural oddities associated with that stretch of coast not least the persistent rumours of the German invasion that was defeated by setting fire to the sea. Then there was the other battle for the skies featuring Her Majesty's own Hawk Division who were charged with intercepting German pigeons carrying messages to and from fifth columnists. MI5 trained an elite battalion of falcons to either kill, or better capture, Himmler's rock dove force. At least two were held in a POW coop before being retrained as double agents to spread disinformation back in Germany.

Finally Carl, whose name still appears on utility bills despite the fact he really did disappear some time ago. Periodically one of the companies concerned is approached about changing the name on the bill but they always insist that Carl needs to contact them. When it's pointed out that Carl is missing and very probably dead they respond by saying that Carl must phone the Southampton office. Presumably this is where the psychic call centre workers who commune with dead people are employed and it would be nice to confirm this if anyone knows. In the meantime though Carl remains earthbound, kept live through an electricity summons in south east London and for him, life truly is a gas (bill).

☞ SUBSCRIBE

The three 2007 editions of One Eye Grey, Transpontine Drift, Goose in Southwark and Orbital are available for £9.00 online including postage and free mystery book while stocks last.

Visit www.fandmpublications.co.uk for details.

☞ CONTRIBUTE

F&M Publications welcomes contributions of short stories based on folktales or ghost stories, or even just weird tales with a London setting. Be creative, be playful, be horrible, but be London even if we've taken liberties this time.

☞ ADVERTISE

One Eye Grey does not sell advertising in the traditional sense but does welcome sponsors for sentences or paragraphs. You can also, if you like, insert yourself or a loved one into the stories as a character. Further details on the website. At the end of One Eye Grey there will be an acknowledgment of your generous donation. So in this edition: Crockatt and Powell of Lower Marsh Street SE 1 come up with enough for page sixteen and the Catalyst Club Brighton (www.catalyst-club.com) covered pages twelve and thirteen. The marvelous Stardust (www.stardustkids.co.uk) of Herne Hill did us proud for the second paragraph on page nineteen and Atlantis Books of Museum Street (www.theatlantisbookshop.com) couldn't decide on a sentence or page so magically covered every time we used the words that and zoo. Ben's photo fees were happily covered by those purveyors of stress relief Breath London whose website is, deep breath please, www.holisticbodyworkstherapies.com. Niceties Tokens (www.team-nice.co.uk) in a fit chivalry opened the doors for page forty one and Martik Jewellery (www.martickjewellery.com) made page sixty two sparkle.